Kenn Viselman presents...

Li'l Pet Hospital™

THE VERY RAINY DAY

Created by Kenn Viselman

Written by Scott Stabile and Catherine Lyon

HarperEntertainment

An Imprint of HarperCollins*Publishers*

ISBN 0-06-054838-X

First printing: July 2003

Visit HarperEntertainment on the World Wide Web at
www.harpercollins.com

10 9 8 7 6 5 4 3 2 1

Dear Parents:

The most wonderful thing in children's lives is the love they receive from their families. Children derive tremendous pleasure from imitating their parents' care in pretend play and make-believe.

The Li'l Pets in Healy Fields are much like young children in their high spirits, rambunctiousness, and curiosity, as well as in their need to be loved and nurtured. They spend their days playing games, sharing stories, and exploring the world around them. When the adventures are just too much for the Li'l Pets to handle by themselves, the delightful Dr. Foxx is always there to fix their boo-boos and make them feel well and happy again. Then all they need is a li'l extra love from you.

Welcome to the loving and lovable world of the Li'l Pet Hospital!

With all good wishes,

Kenn Viselman

One day at the Li'l Pet Hospital, Scuffs the Kitten was looking at herself in the mirror. "I look so beautiful today," she said to herself.

Then Dr. Foxx came in with some good news.

"Good morning, Scuffs. It seems to me,
Your cold is gone. Now you are free,
To run along your merry way,
And play the way that kittens play!"

5

"I *knew* I was looking especially lovely this morning," said Scuffs. "Thank you, Dr. Foxx."

Scuffs hopped out of bed and skipped outside. Then she ran right to her favorite fence, jumped up, and began to prance back and forth.

Oh, how she loved to spin and whirl, twirling her long and lovely tail in the air.

Tired from all her prancing and dancing, Scuffs decided it was time for a little beauty rest. But just as she settled down, she heard a very loud rumble.

She looked up and saw dark gray clouds in the sky. Suddenly . . . *splat, splat, splat* . . . she felt large wet drops on her head.

"Oh, my!"
said Scuffs.
"It's starting to rain.
My soft brown fur
will be ruined!"

She jumped
down from
the fence
and ran under
a big oak
tree to
keep dry.

She curled up into a ball and hid under a giant leaf.

"I think I'll just take my catnap here until the rain stops," she purred.

Scuffs was fast asleep when suddenly . . . *splat, splat, splat* . . . the rain was leaking through the leaf and Scuffs was getting wet. "Oh, my my! My beautiful fur!"

Scuffs ran to her friend Splint the Bunny's home. Splint lived underground. I do hope it's dry there, thought Scuffs.

"Lovely Splint," said Scuffs. "May I stay with you until this nasty rain stops? I need a dry place to get my beauty rest."

"Sure, Scuffs. And after your nap we can play together!" cried Splint with excitement.

Scuffs and Splint had just sat down in Splint's living room when once again . . . *splat, splat, splat* . . . the rain was leaking into Splint's burrow.

"Oh, my. Oh, my," said Scuffs.
"The rain is getting in here, too.
My beautiful paws are getting
muddy!"

"Come on, Scuffs," said Splint. "Let's go to Filo's house. It must be dry there!" The two friends rushed to Filo the Lion Cub's tree house.

Pots and pans were scattered
everywhere to catch all the rain
that was dripping in. Filo even had a
frying pan over his head to stay dry.

"What fun!" said Splint. "Let's see who can catch the most water in a pan!"

"Oh, Splint, you manage to find fun in everything," said Filo.

19

"This isn't fun for me," cried Scuffs.
"My spotted fur is damp and my
perfect paws are muddy. This just
won't do!"

The three pets hurried off to their
friend Cutie Pie's home. Cutie Pie
the Giraffe had a big house and
would certainly have room for a
few guests.

"Hello, sweet friends, please do come in. I just finished painting a picture of the rainstorm and was about to take a nap. Care to join me?" asked Cutie Pie.

"A beauty nap! Delightful!" purred Scuffs.

"Well, I just ate, so I *am* a little sleepy," said Filo.

"I'm tired from hopping through all those rain puddles, so that sounds fine to me, too," added Splint.

The friends all lay down and curled up into their favorite sleeping positions.

They were almost asleep
when suddenly…
SNORE,
SNORE,
SNORE!
Cutie Pie was
snoring the
loudest
snores that
any of them
had
ever
heard!

Scuffs, Filo, and Splint jumped
up. "I'll never get my beauty rest
like this!" cried Scuffs. "What are
we going to do?"

Then Splint had an idea. "I know just the place where we can all stay dry *and* take a nap," she said to her friends.

Scuffs, Filo, and Splint whispered
good-bye to Cutie Pie and headed into
the rain once more. Scuffs couldn't
wait to see what Splint had in mind.

"At last," purred Scuffs, when she saw where they were headed. "We can all take a beauty nap now."

"Right," said Splint with a smile. "And you'll be warm and dry and won't have to worry about a thing."

The three friends curled up together in the one spot that would protect them from the rain . . . under their friend Stomp the Elephant, who didn't mind the rain at all! Finally, all the pet friends were as comfy as could be.

And now all they need is

30

a li'l extra love from you!

Dr. Foxx says:

If you come down with a cold,
Try to do as you are told.

Drink lots of water, get plenty of rest,
And once again you'll feel your best.

Now give your pet some loving care,
And take her out for a little fresh air.